I Am Belle

By Andrea Posner-Sanchez
Illustrated by Alan Batson

 A GOLDEN BOOK • NEW YORK

 Published in the United States by Golden Books, an imprint of Random House Children's Books, a division of Penguin Random House LLC, 1745 Broadway, New York, NY 10019, and in Canada by Penguin Random House Canada Limited, Toronto, in conjunction with Disney Enterprises, Inc. Golden Books, A Golden Book, A Little Golden Book, the G colophon, and the distinctive gold spine are registered trademarks of Penguin Random House LLC.
randomhousekids.com
ISBN 978-0-7364-3905-3 (trade) — ISBN 978-0-7364-3906-0 (ebook)
Printed in the United States of America
10 9 8 7 6 5 4 3 2

I am
Belle.

I live in a small
house in a small town.

This is my father, *Maurice*.

He's an inventor.

Some of his inventions look a little strange. I love that Papa sees things in ways that others don't.

Living in our town is nice, but every day is exactly the same.

I feed the animals . . .

. . . tend the gardens,

and shop at the markets.

My favorite place to go is
the village bookshop.

I've read all of the books in
the store—some more than once.

The girls in town think I'm odd because I'd rather read than

SWOOn . . .

. . . over *Gaston*.
They think he's
so handsome.
Gaston agrees!

I can be very **brave**.
When my father went missing,
I raced into the woods and found
him locked up in a mysterious
castle by a creature called the Beast.
I offered to take my father's place as
the Beast's prisoner.

The castle was a strange and scary place filled with talking furniture! Luckily, I am good at making new friends.

I met a clock named *Cogsworth*, a candelabrum named *Lumiere*, a teapot named *Mrs. Potts*, and her son, *Chip*, a teacup.

I missed my father terribly and was in no mood to eat. But being served delicious food by singing and dancing silverware cheered me right up!

Sometimes I can be **too curious** for my own good. Even though the Beast told me not to, I went to the West Wing of the castle and saw an *enchanted rose*.

I am comfortable around all creatures, including little birds,

big

horses . . .

. . . and even *enchanted footstools* that act like dogs.

Can you guess
which room in the
Beast's castle
I like the
most?

The library, of course!

I can bring out the best in people—
and beasts. Once the Beast's caring
nature came out, he became my
favorite dance partner.

Thanks to the love I had for the Beast, the curse that had been placed on everyone in his castle was lifted! They all became human again. That chapter of my life was more exciting than any in my favorite books!